Disney's
American Frontier #

SACAJAWEA AND THE JOURNEY TO THE PACIFIC

A Historical Novel

By Gina Ingoglia
Illustrations by Charlie Shaw
Cover illustration by Dave Henderson

DISNEY PRESS
NEW YORK

Look for these other books in the
American Frontier series:

Calamity Jane at Fort Sanders

Davy Crockett and the Creek Indians

Davy Crockett and the Highwaymen

Davy Crockett and the King of the River

Davy Crockett and the Pirates at Cave-in Rock

Davy Crockett at the Alamo

Johnny Appleseed and the Planting of the West

FIRST EDITION
1   3   5   7   9   10   8   6   4   2

Library of Congress Catalog Card Number: 92-52977
ISBN: 1-56282-262-4/1-56282-263-2 (lib. bdg.)

Consultant: Judith A. Brundin, Supervisory Education Specialist
National Museum of the American Indian
Smithsonian Institution, New York

PACIFIC O.

WASHINGTON

COLUMBIA R.

PORTLAND

OREGON

SNAKE

SALMON

IDAHO

JEFFERSON R.

MONTANA

MISSOURI R.

GREAT FALLS

THREE FORKS

GALLATIN R.

MADISON R.

NORTH
DAKOTA

BISMARCK

N

0   50   100   150 MILES

CHAPTER 1

Many years ago, before white men knew her land well, a young girl was busy gathering pine nuts for the winter. Her name was Grass Maiden.

The nuts grew inside pine cones that hung from the branches of an old piñon tree. Many of the egg-shaped cones had already dropped to the ground. The young girl stood on tiptoe and knocked more off with a long wooden pole.

"Watch out, Happy Song—here they come!" Grass Maiden warned her friend, swinging the pole wildly above her head. The cones tumbled down onto the hard ground. Happy Song quickly picked them up. She broke them apart and shook them over a basket woven from cattail reeds. The half-inch-long nuts, which looked like seeds, fell into the basket.

Both girls had straight black hair tied in neat braids. They wore soft deerskin dresses and leggings carefully embroidered with some porcupine quills. Their short rabbit-skin capes kept out the frosty air. Moss-lined moccasins covered their bare feet.

"I have left plenty of cones at the top of the tree," said Grass Maiden, "for the nuthatches."

"I wish we could leave them *all* for the birds," said

Happy Song. "I really hate pine nut mush."

Grass Maiden stopped to catch her breath. She gazed around at the wide valley walled in by the Mountains of No Summer, mountains where cold and ice always remained. In the late afternoon light, the snowy peaks glowed pink.

Grass Maiden's village was a half-hour's walk away. She sighed as she looked at the smoke curling from the openings in the roofs of the longhouses. Another long winter in the valley lay ahead.

Happy Song and Grass Maiden were people living in the Great Basin, near the Plains. They belonged to the Shoshone tribe. Their own families, along with several others, had recently moved near the valley in the Plains.

During the other seasons, the families lived across the flatlands and mountains. They moved on horseback, following buffalo herds, fishing in the rivers, and gathering nuts and roots.

In winter, the Shoshones stayed in villages. As many as ten families lived side by side in a village. They shared food and tried to keep warm through the long season of icy winds and snow.

Grass Maiden knelt next to Happy Song and helped her gather nuts off the ground.

"You hate pine nut mush," said Grass Maiden. "*I* hate spending the winter in the valley! Most of the families are here, and soon it will snow. Then we will all be living close together for months. Remember last winter, when Red Feather's baby cried every night, and all day, too!"

"I saw her yesterday," said Happy Song. "She's walking now."

"Was she crying?" asked Grass Maiden.

Happy Song giggled.

"No," she said. "She was just walking."

Grass Maiden saw a reddish brown bird high in the sky. Her heart jumped: She'd spotted a giant golden eagle! It was an honor for her to see this creature. It was one of the Shoshones' sacred animals.

"Look!" Grass Maiden called, and pointed to the bird.

Together the girls watched the eagle glide on the wind, high above the valley floor. With its wide wings glistening in the sun, the bird turned and veered west over the mountains.

"I'd like to fly like that!" said Grass Maiden.

"Not me," said Happy Song. "I would be afraid to be so high above the ground."

Grass Maiden closed her eyes and spread her arms. On her make-believe wings, she pretended she was skimming through the chilly air, over the Mountains of No Summer, away from the village. She flew along the Big River, to the west. Her father had told her many times about the river and its great power: "I have seen its waters tumble," he'd told Grass Maiden. "Our strongest canoes were tossed and sucked down into the whirlpools as if they were floating leaves."

In her imaginary journey, Grass Maiden flew toward the sunset, following the Big River. Before her closed eyes, she saw the Never-Ending Waters. Her father had never seen it, but Grass Maiden knew it was there. Others had seen it.

"Dear Grass Maiden," asked a gentle voice, "are you going to fly away and leave us all behind?"

Grass Maiden lowered her arms and turned around. A kind-looking old man smiled at her. She smiled back.

"I wish I *could* be a bird and fly," she said.

The old man wore a deerskin shirt and leggings. With one hand, he held a heavy buffalo robe slung over his shoulders.

Deep lines, caused by years of sun and wind, etched his face. The old man's back was no longer straight, and he walked with a stick. He'd lived longer than anyone else in the village. Because of this, he had earned the name Father of Many Winters. The children called him Old Father.

"Where would you go?" he asked Grass Maiden.

"I want to see the Never-Ending Waters," she said.

"That is very far away," said Old Father. "They say the water has a strange taste. I have always wanted to see it myself. Why don't we fly away together?"

Grass Maiden laughed.

"We might see the powerful sea creatures who live in the Never-Ending Waters," said the old man. "I hear they are of great size and spray water from their heads."

"How big are they?" asked Grass Maiden.

"Much bigger than our large canoes," said Old Father.

Bigger than huge canoes! Grass Maiden could hardly believe what she heard. But it must be so if Old Father said it.

Old Father turned to Happy Song, who now stood quietly next to him. "And what about you, Happy Song?" he asked. "Would you like to join us?"

Before Happy Song could answer, a boy on a brown-and-white pony trotted up to them. He was Grass Maiden's brother, older than her by two years. As always, he was in a hurry. Without stopping, he rode past, calling out to her.

"Little sister," he said, "it will be getting dark soon, and you are supposed to come home."

Then the boy saw Old Father. He jumped off his pony and ran over to him.

"I have forgotten my manners, Old Father," he said. "I should have spoken to you first. I hope you are well."

Old Father nodded. "Thank you, Cameahwait," he said.

The boy smiled. He ran to his pony, jumped on its back, kicked the animal's sides with his heels, and galloped off.

"Cameahwait—One Who Never Walks—is well named," said Old Father. "Instead of walking, he runs. Instead of running, he rides a pony. He is strong and people like him. I can tell now: He will be a chief. One day, if he does something brave, he may get a new name. But for now, One Who Never Walks suits him well."

Grass Maiden sighed. She wished *she* had a different name. Grass Maiden! What kind of name was that for a girl who wanted to fly across the Mountains of No Summer and see the Never-Ending Waters? But she knew she could never complain. She'd been named by her grandmother, who had chosen her name with care.

Because Old Father was wise, sometimes it seemed to Grass Maiden that he could read her thoughts.

"And your name, Boinaiv—Grass Maiden—suits you," he said. "You are full of life, just like the grass. Grass is always stirring with small creatures. It provides a home for them. Grass provides food for our sacred buffalo, who give so much to us. Many birds you like build their nests in the grass."

"But grass stays on the earth," said Grass Maiden. "A bird can leave the land. It can fly."

Old Father took Grass Maiden by the hand.

"Listen carefully to me," he said. "Someday you will do something you can't even dream of now. At first you will think it is bad. But it will be good. Wait and see."

Old Father looked at the sky. "It will snow tonight," he told the girls. "Gather up the rest of those pine nuts before you go home. By morning everything will be covered deep in snow.

"I must start back now," he continued. "The sun will be setting soon. Your young legs can carry you to the village with ease. They are strong like a young deer's. It takes me longer to walk. My legs have grown stiff with age, like an old elk's."

Old Father walked slowly away. Grass Maiden and Happy Song got back to work and collected the rest of the nuts. They lifted the basket by its handles and, carrying it between them, walked home.

"I have been thinking," said Happy Song. "Next summer, we will be old enough to go out on our vision quest—to find our guardian spirits. Because you love birds so much, maybe your guardian spirit will be a bird!"

Grass Maiden shivered with both excitement and fear. Her vision quest! After she found her guardian spirit, she would no longer be looked upon as a child but as a young Shoshone woman.

Of course, she looked forward to it. Every girl did. But as part of her vision quest, she had to spend a night all alone in the Mountains of No Summer. While she was alone, she would fast. She would remain naked in the cold, denying her body any comfort. If a spirit took pity on her, it would appear and help her. The spirit often took the form of an animal. For the rest of her life, she would be able to call on it to guide her and assist her in times of danger.

Grass Maiden smiled at Happy Song. "I hope with all my heart," she said, "that my guardian spirit will be a bird!"

It snowed all night. In the morning, when Grass Maiden woke up, a frozen white blanket lay thick over the valley. She got up from beneath her warm buffalo robe and walked over to the fire. Then she helped her mother prepare roasted bitter-root, dried buffalo meat, and smoked fish for the morning meal.

"Old Father said it would snow," said Grass Maiden.

"The sky is as gray as a wolf's fur," said her mother. "Another snowfall, greater than this one, is coming. Your father and Cameahwait are getting the horses. We will keep them in here with us until the storm passes. It is a danger to be out in a blizzard, even for a horse."

Grass Maiden frowned. Another storm was coming. Her mother touched her on the shoulder and smiled.

"I know you don't like the winter in the village," she said. "But that is no reason to look sad."

Grass Maiden smiled. "I know," she said. "But I'd rather be outside, picking huckleberries or currants...."

"Or chasing rabbits," said her mother. "Remember last spring when you fell in the mud? That was so funny. Cameahwait laughed so long and hard."

Grass Maiden grinned. "But I caught the rabbit!" she said.

"You will have a busy winter, anyway," said her mother. "You and I have so much to do before springtime comes."

The cold months slowly passed. Grass Maiden helped her mother mend torn fishnets and repair broken baskets. Cameahwait also helped to prepare for the rest of the year. He and his father sharpened their spears and fashioned sinew-backed bows and stone arrowheads for hunting.

During dreary snowy days, when her mother didn't need her help, Grass Maiden sat next to the fire with Happy Song and the other children and listened to storytellers.

In the long evening hours, the Shoshone families gathered together and held religious ceremonies. They played music and sang and danced. But it was smoky and stuffy. The children grew noisy and bored. And Grass Maiden couldn't wait for spring!

CHAPTER 2

L ittle by little, the days grew warmer and longer. Icicles dripped. The blanket of snow melted away. In its place, pale blue camas flowers, shaped like tiny stars, covered the valley. And early one morning, Grass Maiden heard the clear whistlelike song of a bird. A meadowlark was choosing its nesting territory. It was spring.

At last, the time had come for the Shoshones to leave. The families had had enough of village life and were eager to move out to the Plains and the rivers. Some would travel in groups and set up camps together. Others would go their separate ways.

Grass Maiden helped her family pack their belongings. Her father attached a large sled, or travois, to the back of one of their horses. The animal would drag it, loaded with the family's supplies, from camp to camp.

Grass Maiden and Cameahwait helped to load the sled. They carried out folded mats and poles from the longhouses, as well as hides to make tipis. Their mother handed them clothes, baskets, bowls, special tools for making arrowheads, soft rabbit-fur blankets, and digging sticks with T-shaped handles made from elk antlers.

Cameahwait proudly carried out a fishing spear and handed it to his father. "I am looking forward to fishing at Three Forks," Cameahwait said. "I hope to catch a big one!"

"If not this summer, you will the next," said his father. "The fish have always been good to us there."

Happy Song came over to watch. Her family was also heading for the fishing grounds at Three Forks.

"Father said to tell you we are almost ready," she said.

"We will be ready soon, too," said Grass Maiden's father.

A while later, the remaining families set off on horseback, leaving the village behind until fall.

They followed a narrow river that flowed from the valley all the way to the fishing grounds at Three Forks. Grass Maiden's and Happy Song's ponies trotted side by side.

The third day out, the families stopped at a marsh. The women set up camp while the men hunted for game. Grass Maiden, Happy Song, and the other children made baskets and searched for duck eggs and ferns.

"Let's look in those grasses close to the marsh," said Grass Maiden. "We found some eggs there last year."

"I have been looking forward to this hunt all winter," said Happy Song. "Especially when I was eating pine nut mush!"

Grass Maiden laughed.

"It's too bad," she said, "that eggs can't be kept all year like other foods."

"I know," said Happy Song. "I'd eat one every day!"

As they walked into the marsh, a male duck with a gleaming dark green head flew above them. Then a plain brown duck burst from the grasses and flew away.

"We have startled her," said Happy Song. "The nest must be close by."

They looked on the ground and found the nest, a hidden, shallow bowl of grass. It was lined with fluffy, soft feathers the duck had plucked from her breast. The nest held ten pale greenish brown eggs.

"This duck is generous to us," said Grass Maiden. "But we cannot take too many eggs. We must leave some for her."

She and Happy Song each took two eggs. Then they searched around for more duck nests and picked bright green fiddlehead ferns. They chose the new ferns that grew tightly coiled and close to the ground. In a few days, the ferns left behind would unwind into feathery fronds, some as tall as Grass Maiden's father. When their baskets were full, Grass Maiden and Happy Song carried the eggs and ferns back to camp. That night, their families feasted.

After a week or two at the marsh, it was time to move along. They were all riding one morning when Grass Maiden noticed a familiar large rock in the distance. Against the sky, it looked like the head of a huge beaver.

"Look!" she said, pointing it out to Happy Song. "I can see Beaverhead Rock! That means we're not far from Three Forks."

"I can't wait," Happy Song said. "I'm tired of traveling."

The families reached Three Forks two days later. At Three Forks, three rivers came together to form one. It was very long and flowed east, toward the land of the sunrise.

Three Forks was a good place to fish, and, on the plains, buffalo and antelope were plentiful.

The women set up tipis by fastening buffalo hides on to tall poles. Along the river, the men constructed wooden fishing platforms. Grass Maiden helped put together the drying racks, where the cleaned fish would hang, suspended above small fires. The smoke preserved the fish and gave it a good flavor. Some of the fish would be eaten as soon as it was smoked. The rest would be stored in baskets.

The late spring passed quickly, and the long days of early summer came to Three Forks.

"Grass Maiden," said her mother one morning. "There are great numbers of fish this year. We need reeds to make more baskets for them. This morning, I saw many cattails growing along the river, down near the falls. Why don't you and Happy Song gather some."

Then Grass Maiden's mother gave them a warning.

"You must be careful," she said. "I hear the young Hidatsa warriors have come again from the east. They like to prove they are strong by carrying off young girls!"

Around a bend in the river, Grass Maiden and Happy Song found a good spot to gather reeds. The water was shallow enough for wading. But downstream, the river suddenly dropped into a crashing waterfall.

The girls spoke very little. The roar of the falls drowned out their voices. They gathered the cattails along one bank and decided to wade to the other side.

Happy Song reached the opposite bank. But halfway across the river, Grass Maiden stopped. She noticed a tall white egret wading by the shore. The bird probed the muddy bottom with its long bill, searching for fish. Then Grass Maiden heard her friend scream.

"Run, Grass Maiden!" she cried. "Run!"

Happy Song pointed to a clump of trees. There, in the leafy shadows, five men sat silently on horseback, watching the two girls. Grass Maiden's heart jumped.

The men yelled, urging their horses on, and the excited

animals plunged into the water. Two men chased Happy Song.
The other three went after Grass Maiden. The girls fled in
two directions. Happy Song quickly disappeared into a tangle
of tall weeds. Caught in the middle of the river, Grass Maiden
struggled to the shore.

Grass Maiden looked quickly over her shoulder. Out of
the corner of her eye, she saw Happy Song crawl into a low
cave, hidden behind a thorny gooseberry thicket. She's
escaped! thought Grass Maiden.

Grass Maiden struggled through the water. She slipped
on an underwater rock and fell flat. Dripping, she got to her
feet and scrambled to the riverbank. She didn't know where
to go, so she ran into a grove of young pines. The short bushy
trees were growing close together. Perhaps they might slow
down the horses!

When Grass Maiden ran out of the far side of the grove,
the braves were no longer right behind her. She spotted a large
boulder and quickly hid behind it.

On her knees, Grass Maiden bent her head down, trying
to be as small as possible. She was soaking wet. She felt her
heart thumping hard in her chest. It beat so fast and loud, she
thought the men might hear it! If she hadn't stopped to watch
that bird, she thought, she might have escaped with Happy
Song.

Minutes passed. No one came. Grass Maiden waited
some more. Still, there was no sound of horses or men.
Perhaps she'd gotten away. Then a twig snapped next to her.

Slowly Grass Maiden looked up. A warrior on horseback
gave her an eerie smile. He'd probably been there a long time.
Grass Maiden hadn't escaped, after all.

CHAPTER 3

The braves carried Grass Maiden far from Three Forks. They rode beside the long river toward the land of the sunrise.

Grass Maiden thought only of escape, but her captors never took their eyes off her. At night, they tied her ankles together with a strip of long leather. She could get around, but she couldn't run.

Each night, Grass Maiden lay awake, watching the stars and thinking of home. She heard the warriors talking and joking among themselves. If she could only understand their language. Were they talking about her? Would she be beaten? Would she be a slave?

Then the day that she dreaded came. One afternoon, the long journey ended. They had arrived at a Hidatsa village.

Grass Maiden had never seen anything like it. These people didn't live together in longhouses like the Shoshones did. Their lodges looked like great overturned bowls covered with thick roofs of earth. Smoke from camp fires curled out of holes in the center of the roofs.

The warriors took her inside one of the lodges. Coming out of the bright sunlight, she had trouble seeing well in the dim room. She managed to make out several women sitting next to a flickering fire. The warriors said something to them, pushed Grass Maiden in their direction, and left.

One woman slowly rose to her feet and came over to her. She was old but looked strong. She took Grass Maiden firmly by the hand and led her away from the other women. When they were alone, the woman spoke—in Shoshone.

"What is your name?" she asked Grass Maiden, still holding her hand. "You are a Shoshone girl?"

Grass Maiden nodded. "My name is Grass Maiden."

The woman smiled but looked sad all the same.

"I am Running Fox," she said. "I too am Shoshone. I was taken from my people when I was your age." She sighed and continued, "Even now that I am old I think of my home. The pain of being away from my people never passes. In my heart I will always be a Shoshone.

"But I want you to know something," she went on. "These people will not be cruel to you. It will not be easy living here, but it will not be so hard."

"Is there no way I can go home?" asked Grass Maiden.

Running Fox smiled her sad smile. "The young Hidatsa braves have captured many girls," she said. "Some ran away, but they were always brought back."

She went to the fire, picked up a bowl of cooked corn, and handed it to Grass Maiden.

"Eat this, dear girl," she said. "Then rest."

Grass Maiden took the bowl and ate the corn with her fingers. She stretched out on a buffalo robe and tried to sleep, but instead daydreamed about running away. Where would she go? she wondered. And what if she got captured by someone else and ended up worse off than she was! So, even though it was hard, she decided to put plans of escape out of her mind.

As best she could, Grass Maiden became a part of the village life. Whenever buffalo came near the villages, the Hidatsa men rode out and hunted them on horseback. Grass Maiden helped the women and girls in the fields. She dug holes with a sharp stick and planted beans, squash, pumpkins, and corn.

Grass Maiden also fished. The women took her out on the river in round bull boats made of buffalo hides stretched over frames of bent willow wood.

At night, she sat with Running Fox and some of the women. Little by little, she learned to speak Hidatsa. But in her heart, Grass Maiden would always be a Shoshone.

One morning a young boy came to her with a message. "Our chief wishes to see you," he said. "Right away."

Grass Maiden followed the boy to the chief's large lodge.

"You live with us now, not the Shoshones," the chief said to her. "Grass Maiden is a Shoshone name. From this day on, you will answer to a Hidatsa name. Our warriors say when they found you, you were looking at a large white bird. Your name is to be Sacajawea—Bird Woman."

Bird Woman! Grass Maiden was torn. She liked her new name, but how could she answer to a name given to her by people who had kidnapped her from her family?

But then she thought of Father of Many Winters. He'd said something would happen to her that she'd never dreamed of. He said it would seem bad, but it would be good. Perhaps this is what he meant.

Grass Maiden decided to accept her new name. From that moment on, she was Sacajawea.

CHAPTER 4

As the sun and the moon crossed the heavens many times, the seasons changed. Sacajawea changed as well and grew into a young woman.

The time for her vision quest passed her by. Without a vision quest she could not fully complete the passage from being a child to becoming a woman. And more than anything, in spirit as well as body, she wished to be a Shoshone woman.

Late one fall, she noticed a strange-looking man around the village. She'd never seen anyone like him; he was heavier than the other men, and his skin was lighter. At night, he would visit with the chief.

One warm evening, Sacajawea and an old woman were outside, filling deerskin sacks with dried beans. The stranger walked by. As he passed Sacajawea, he smiled at her.

"Who is he?" she asked the old woman.

"He lives close to the Mandans across the river," she told Sacajawea. "His mother came from a tribe far away. I do not know about his father."

The old woman smiled.

"The Mandans say he boasts," she said. "They call him funny names—like Great Horse from Afar."

Sacajawea smiled back.

"What does he do?" asked Sacajawea. "I see him go into the chief's lodge at night with other men."

But the old woman had had enough talk.

"Stop asking so many questions, Sacajawea," she said. "The chief likes to play gambling games with him, that's all. The man's presence means nothing to you."

Two nights later, Sacajawea was called into the chief's lodge. She saw the strange man was there, too.

"It is time you were a wife," the chief told Sacajawea. "This man would like you to live with him."

Sacajawea was shocked. She didn't want to marry this man, this Great Horse from Afar! When she was very little, her parents had chosen a Shoshone man, a man named Blue Feather, who would someday be her husband. If she were back home, she would be married to him. But now she had no choice. The chief's word was always obeyed.

"When am I to leave?" she asked the chief.

"He will take you with him tonight," said the chief. "I see no reason for you to delay. Do you?"

Sacajawea sighed and shook her head. No, there was no reason. She went back to the lodge and gathered up her few belongings—a buffalo robe, a bowl, and a digging stick were all she owned. And she still had a string of blue glass beads from her Shoshone days. She had been carrying them on the day she was captured, and in all the time that followed, she'd taken care never to lose them.

"Where are you going, Sacajawea?" asked Running Fox, seeing her carrying the load.

"I am to be the stranger's wife," she answered. She could hardly believe her own words. She had always wanted to leave

the village, but she never thought it would be like this.

"I will miss you," said Running Fox.

Sacajawea smiled at her. "You have been a good friend," she said.

Some of the women gathered around to say good-bye and wish her well. Sacajawea liked them, but except for Running Fox, she'd hadn't made any close friends. She'd never been one of them. And even though her future was unsure, she felt happy to leave the Hidatsa village behind her.

She followed the man down to the river. He pointed to a dugout canoe he'd left on the shore.

"That's mine," he said. "I built it myself."

Sacajawea loaded the buffalo robe into the boat and laid the digging stick on top. She climbed in, and the man handed her one of the paddles lying in the dugout. He pushed the boat into the water and hopped in.

As they paddled across the river, Sacajawea asked him his name.

"Toussaint Charbonneau," he said.

"What kind of name is that?" she asked. She thought of what the Mandans called him and tried not to smile.

"It is French," he explained. "Long ago, my father's people came from a faraway place called France. Now they live in a land north of here called Canada. I'm a fur trapper. I trade animal skins with Indian traders."

"Who are the Indians?" asked Sacajawea.

Charbonneau laughed.

"Who are the Indians!" he said. "You—your people are the Indian people!"

Charbonneau stopped paddling for a minute.

"I never thought of it before," he said to Sacajawea. "I

guess you wouldn't know. It's a name white people gave you."

As they reached the shore, Charbonneau pointed to a house of logs set back in a clearing.

"That's my cabin—our cabin," he said. "I built it myself."

Sacajawea looked at her new home.

"You must have very strong arms, Charbonneau," she said, "to lift those logs alone."

Charbonneau threw back his head and laughed out loud.

"Alone!" he hooted. "Thank you for thinking I am as strong as ten bears."

Sacajawea hid her smile behind her hand.

"I thought you said you built it yourself," she said.

Charbonneau was a little annoyed; he wasn't used to being teased.

"That is just a way of talking," he said. "Of course I didn't build it myself. I traded some furs with the Mandans. They helped me build it."

Sacajawea moved into the log cabin with Charbonneau. He was kind to her, and she grew to like him. And when he boasted too much, she teased him a little. In the evenings, he taught her new words in languages spoken by white men. She decided not to tell him about the husband her parents had chosen for her. What good would it do, and besides, she would probably never see that man again.

Almost a year passed. One day Sacajawea told Charbonneau she was going to have a baby. The child would be born in winter.

CHAPTER 5

Freezing weather came early that year. Brisk breezes rippled the river, and crusts of thin ice appeared at the water's edge. Every morning, curtains of mist hung above the choppy waves.

One cold, gray day, Sacajawea went to the river to collect water. She carried a wooden bucket with a rope handle.

A fallen tree, with one end jutting into the water, lay on the shore. Sacajawea inched her way out along the partially submerged, icy trunk. As she was about to dip the bucket into the river, she heard a flock of honking wild geese.

She looked up and saw several boats coming upstream.

Sacajawea made her way off the log and hurried ashore. Hiding, she watched the boats pass by. They were filled with white men!

When Sacajawea got a closer look at their faces, she was amazed. No two white men looked alike. Some had long bushy hair growing out of their faces and on their chins. Others had bare faces. One man's hair was reddish and shiny, the color of copper. Another's was pale yellow and fine, like silk growing inside an ear of corn. And one man was different from the others. His skin was not white but dark brown, his hair black.

Still hidden by the tangles of brush growing along the river, Sacajawea followed on the bank, alongside the boats.

The men pulled ashore and dragged the boats up onto the bank. To warm up, several of them rubbed their arms and stamped their feet on the frozen ground.

A few of the men wore hide clothes like Charbonneau's. All of the other men were dressed the same. They wore white shirts and blue jackets. White leather straps crossed their chests. Their pants were brown or white, tucked into tall black boots that almost reached their knees. They wore wide black hats rounded at the top like little hills. Two of the men's hats were trimmed with white feathers.

A large black dog with a long tail and floppy ears scrambled out of the biggest boat, startling some waterfowl.

The two men with the feathered hats directed the unloading. Both of them were very tall; one was the man with red hair. While the crew worked, the two men leaned against a boat to talk. Sacajawea silently crept behind a patch of tall cattails and listened. They were speaking in one of the languages of the white man that Charbonneau had taught her. The red-headed man spoke first.

"Well, my friend," he said. "We've done it! And I can't wait to get it down!" He leaned into the boat and lifted out a wooden box. He took out a notebook, a quill pen, and a bottle of ink. Then he opened the notebook and began to write in it. As he wrote, he read aloud:

Today, October 27, 1804, after a long and hard trip of five and a half months, Captain Meriwether Lewis and I along with a crew of 43 brave and good men have reached our winter site on the Missouri River.

We will begin work on the fort as soon as we meet with the Mandan chiefs.

May God bless us all.

Signed,

Capt. William Clark

"You're an unusual man, Clark," said his companion. "Here we all are, completely exhausted and freezing to death, and you look as fresh as morning."

"You'll proudly tell your grandchildren about this day," said Captain Clark.

"Inasmuch as I'm twenty-nine years old, not married, and have no children," said Captain Lewis, "it may prove difficult...."

Captain Clark, four years older than his friend, shook his head in fake exasperation.

The dog, finished scaring the waterfowl, trotted over to Captain Lewis. He sat at his master's feet and looked up.

Captain Lewis smiled.

"You need some exercise, don't you?" he said to the dog. He picked up a stick and threw it far down the shore.

"Go get it, Scannon!" he said.

The dog barked excitedly and took off. In seconds, he was back with the stick in his mouth. Captain Lewis took the stick from his dog and threw it again. This time he threw it right past Sacajawea's hiding place. As Scannon dashed by, he spotted her.

At that moment, a small crowd of curious Mandans appeared on the shore. Scannon looked at them and back at Sacajawea. The Mandan people appeared a lot more interesting than Sacajawea, and he bounded off to investigate.

Sacajawea ran home to tell Charbonneau what she'd seen.

"Charbonneau," she said. "Many white men are at the river. Many boats, too!"

Charbonneau looked surprised.

"White men?" he asked. "Are you sure?"

Sacajawea nodded. "And they wear strange clothes."

Charbonneau put the pelts inside the cabin door.

"You stay here," he said. "I'll go see what's going on."

Sacajawea waited impatiently. She wished she could have gone along. After all, she was the one who had found the white men.

Charbonneau was gone for almost two hours. When he came back, he was very excited.

"Those men," he said, "they're working for President Thomas Jefferson. They are going to build a fort and spend the winter here. In the spring they will continue upriver."

"Who is President Thomas Jefferson?" asked Sacajawea.

"He's the leader of the United States—this country," explained Charbonneau.

"The men are on a long trip called an expedition," he continued. "They are here to look at the land for President Jefferson. He wants to know about its rivers, mountains, animals, and plants—and the Indians. The men in charge, Captain Lewis and Captain Clark, are following the Missouri River...."

"Is that what white men call the river that flows past our camp?" she asked.

"Yes," said Charbonneau. He continued, "They will go up the Missouri River all the way to its beginning. They will keep on going until they reach the Pacific Ocean."

Before Sacajawea could ask, he began to explain.

"The Pacific Ocean is very big," he said. "Much bigger than a river. You can't see where the water ends."

Sacajawea grew excited. Could he be talking about the Never-Ending Waters? She remembered something Old Father had said about the Never-Ending Waters.

"Does the Pacific Ocean have a strange taste?" she asked.

Charbonneau was surprised. But he was often surprised at what Sacajawea knew. "The taste," he said, "is what the white men call salt. How do you know that?"

Sacajawea was so busy with her own thoughts she didn't answer him. When she was captured by the Hidatsa braves, they had followed the river downstream. It had led them straight to their village. If the explorers were going to follow the Missouri River back upstream to its beginning—to Three Forks—they would be going back to Shoshone country!

"They are going to the land of my people!" she told Charbonneau. She could hardly speak because of her joy.

"I know," said Charbonneau. "They have asked me to go with them. The white men want to set up fur trading with the Indian people. Because they don't speak any Indian languages, I will speak for them. I'll tell you all about it when I get back."

What did he mean, he would tell her all about it when he got back?

"I do not want to *hear* about it," said Sacajawea. "I want to go with you."

Charbonneau laughed.

"*You* go?" he said. "The baby will be born by then."

"I will take the baby with me," said Sacajawea.

Charbonneau became angry. "That is foolish!" he roared. "It is no trip for a child to make. I say you will not go!"

He started for the cabin door.

Sacajawea couldn't believe he was so unfeeling! Couldn't he understand what this meant to her?

"I speak Shoshone," she said to his back. "You cannot. How will you speak to my people for the captains?"

Charbonneau stopped. What she said was true.

"And," added Sacajawea, "when they get to my people's land, they will need horses to cross the Mountains of No Summer. The Shoshones have lots of horses. I can help the white men get some."

Charbonneau knew she was right. He would not be much help with the Shoshones.

"I will speak to them," he said. "Do not expect too much." Then he walked out the cabin door.

Sacajawea could barely wait for his return. If the white men said she could go, she might see her people again.

But hours passed, and Charbonneau didn't come. Sacajawea covered her face with her hands and worried.

Late that evening, Charbonneau came back. He said many of the Mandans agreed with Sacajawea: The white men would have to cross high mountains on horseback. They could not cross by boat. And even though Charbonneau wasn't happy about it, the captains wanted Sacajawea to go on the trip. They knew they would need her help getting horses.

Sacajawea couldn't believe her good fortune. She knew she had to wait through the long winter; the white men weren't leaving for months. Now that she'd be going with them, spring seemed such a long way off.

CHAPTER 6

The sun had just risen, and Sacajawea had already finished eating. She watched Charbonneau chew a mouthful of smoked meat. He swallowed it and looked at her.

"Why do you stare like a wolf about to pounce?" he asked.

"You are taking too long," she said. "The white men are back at work on their fort. The woods are already filled with the sounds of their axes. I will go watch them alone if you do not hurry."

"You will not go without me," said Charbonneau. "You will wait until I am finished."

He picked up a tin cup of hot coffee and drank from it. "Now," he said, "we can go."

Before he got up, Sacajawea was already at the door.

They walked downriver to the campsite the white men had chosen. Crowds of excited Mandan men, women, and children were already there watching the white men build the fort.

Sometimes, during the work, Captain Lewis talked with Charbonneau and Sacajawea.

"Some of your men are very experienced with tools," said Charbonneau. "I should know. I know a lot about building."

"He built our cabin himse—" began Sacajawea.

Charbonneau stared hard at her, and she stopped speaking.

"I chose my men for their various skills," said the captain. "And several, as you say, are experienced with tools." He nodded at a sturdy-looking man who was working nearby. "Sergeant Gass, over there, is a fine carpenter."

"What will the fort look like?" asked Charbonneau.

"We are building two rows of long log houses with slanted roofs," said Captain Lewis. "Each house will have four rooms."

Then he put his hands together and formed an L. "The two buildings will be joined together like this," he explained.

The explorers worked for three weeks. By mid-November, they finished the fort. They called it Fort Mandan.

Just after they moved into their new winter quarters, the first heavy snow fell. Freezing winds shook the fort's crude walls. The river froze and gripped the white men's boats tight in the ice. To trade food and furs with each other, the Mandan and Hidatsa people crossed the frozen river on dogsleds.

During the short gray days, the captains often met with the Mandan chiefs. Charbonneau and Sacajawea went along to interpret.

"Please thank the chiefs for all the food their people have given to us," Captain Lewis said to Charbonneau. "The men brought us half a buffalo and two hundred pounds of meat, and the women gave us bushels of corn."

Charbonneau spoke with the chiefs. Then he spoke to Captain Lewis. "The chiefs are grateful to you as well," he said. "They thank you for the iron corn mill that you gave to the women. Now they will be able to grind their corn into meal in much less time."

Sometimes the talk turned to the explorers' trip in the spring, going west, up the Missouri River.

"The chiefs say you will see mighty waterfalls," Sacajawea told the captains. "They make the earth tremble. And you will also meet the huge grizzly bears, who live and fish along the rivers."

Late one night in February during a heavy snow, Charbonneau raced into Fort Mandan and pounded on the door to the captains' quarters.

"Good grief, Charbonneau," said Captain Clark. "What are you doing out in this storm? It's below freezing out there! Is anything wrong?"

"It's Sacajawea," said Charbonneau. "Her time has come to have our baby. Something is not right. The baby is taking too long to be born. Will you come?"

"Aren't there any Mandan women who can help?" asked the captain.

"The snow is falling hard. It was all I could do to get to the fort," said Charbonneau. "You and I will have to help bring my baby into this world."

"Why, I wouldn't know what to do," said Captain Clark. "We have medicines, but nothing to aid in childbirth!"

Jussome, one of the white interpreters, overheard the conversation and came up to them.

"Captain Clark, I may be able to help," he said. "Do you have any rattlesnake rattles?"

"Rattles?" asked Charbonneau. "What good are they?"

"If you grind up the rattles in water and give them to your wife, the baby will come," explained Jussome. "Strange as it sounds, I know this is true."

"Never!" said Charbonneau. "I will never give such a thing to Sacajawea."

Captain Clark put his hand on Charbonneau's shoulder.

"Sometimes these remedies work," he said. "I happen to have some rattles that I collected for my wildlife studies."

Charbonneau sighed and nodded.

Captain Clark found the jar of snake rattles, pulled on his fur coat, fastened on a pair of snowshoes, and joined Charbonneau. When the men reached the cabin, the baby still hadn't been born. Captain Clark ground up several rattles and stirred them in a cup of water.

Sacajawea drank it and, ten minutes later, gave birth to a baby boy.

"Those rattles," said Charbonneau. "They really did the trick!"

Sacajawea, lying in bed, smiled weakly at Captain Clark.

"What will you name your son?" Captain Clark asked.

"Back in my homeland, our wise elders chose the babies' names," Sacajawea explained. "But now I will have to think of a fine Shoshone name for—"

Charbonneau interrupted her.

"My son will not have a Shoshone name!" he said. "He will have a French name. He will be called Jean-Baptiste."

Sacajawea looked into Charbonneau's eyes.

"He is also my son," she said. "And I will call him what I choose. There is a good Shoshone name for a baby boy. It is Pompey. I will call our son Pompey."

"Pompey!" scoffed Charbonneau. "What kind of a ridiculous name is that?"

"It sounds fine to me," said Captain Clark. "You could call him Pomp for short."

CHAPTER 7

Wherever Sacajawea went, Pomp went, too. He rode, strapped to his mother's back, in a cradleboard lined with fur and soft, dried mosses.

By the end of February, when the baby was about two weeks old, the freezing weather ended.

Sacajawea and Charbonneau went down to the river to see what was going on. The explorers were chipping ice chunks from their boats and repairing the winter damage.

"And how is little Pomp this morning?" Captain Clark asked, taking a peek at him.

"Jean-Baptiste is fine, Captain," answered Charbonneau.

Captain Clark and Sacajawea smiled at one another.

"Well," said the captain to Charbonneau, "I hope the winter is finally coming to an end."

"You never know," said Charbonneau. "I have seen it snow until May!"

But the winter storms had ended for good. By March, the snow had melted, and small yellow flowers opened on the moosewood bushes.

One morning in early April, Sacajawea looked up and saw a flock of birds with huge black-tipped wings.

"Look," she said to Pomp, who was sound asleep on her back. "The whooping cranes are coming back from their winter hunting grounds."

Flying with their long necks and legs extended, the cranes veered toward the river. And, as their kind had done for thousands of years, the tall water birds settled down among the grasses, where they would build their nests and fish.

"Have the captains said any more about the journey?" Sacajawea asked Charbonneau.

"They will be leaving in just six days," he said.

"That is great news," she said to herself. Then she sighed. "But it is hard to wait. For me, each day will limp by like a wounded deer."

But, instead, Sacajawea was so busy getting ready to leave that the next five days raced by like a deer with four good legs. At dawn on the sixth morning, Charbonneau and Sacajawea, with Pomp strapped to her back, walked down to the river.

Several white men were already there, loading up the biggest boat. Crowds of excited people from the Mandan and Hidatsa villages were watching.

"Are we late?" Charbonneau asked Sergeant Gass, who was looking at a rolled sheet of paper. "Captain Lewis said the loading would begin after sunrise."

"You're on time," said the sergeant. "Our biggest boat—the keelboat—isn't going with us. Some of the men are being sent back downriver. They're taking written reports, along with some other items of interest, back east to President Jefferson in Washington."

"Oh, look, Charbonneau," said Sacajawea. "They are putting some animals on the boat."

As the cargo was loaded aboard, Sergeant Gass checked

his list and read each item aloud: "Wooden boxes packed with Mandan clothing and pottery...mountain ram horns...live insects...pressed leaves from various kinds of plants...four magpies...prairie dogs...."

"Why are they taking those things to President Jefferson?" Sacajawea asked Charbonneau.

"I told you," he said. "There are plants and animals in this part of the country that white men have never seen."

Sacajawea was still puzzled. "But the Mandans' pots and clothes...."

"I have *told* you, Sacajawea," Charbonneau said. "The president wants to know all about the Indians who live here— what they wear, what they eat, everything."

Sacajawea didn't ask any more questions. But it seemed strange—a white man who lived so far away wanting to know so much about them. She decided not to bother about such matters. She was about to start a trip back to her homeland, and nothing was more important than that!

Captain Lewis walked up to the boat. Scannon, his tongue dangling from his mouth, trotted next to him.

"All set, Captain," said Sergeant Gass. "The cargo list is checked off and ready for your signature."

The captain took the cargo list and studied it.

Sergeant Gass took an inkwell and a quill pen from a wooden box on the boat. Then Captain Lewis dipped the pen into the ink. He signed his name and the date:

Capt. Meriwether Lewis, April 7, 1805.

Later that morning, the packed keelboat began its trip back east, downstream on the Missouri. Sacajawea and

Charbonneau stood next to Captain Clark and watched the men load the remaining boats—the two long boats, which they called pirogues, and the six dugout canoes. Their western trip upstream, against the current, was going to be long and hard.

York appeared, carrying a small writing desk piled high with wooden packing cases.

"Where do you want these, Captain?" he asked.

"Good grief, York," said Captain Clark, "you'll break your back carrying all that in one load."

Charbonneau stepped forward to help, but York shook his head. He put the desk lightly down inside the pirogue and stacked the boxes next to it.

"York is very strong," Sacajawea said to Captain Clark. "Most men could not carry so many things."

"York has helped me for years," Captain Clark said. "If I ever get in trouble, I hope he's around to help!"

In two hours, the boats were loaded with axes, medicines, cooking utensils, cases of navigational instruments, books, a microscope, tents, blankets, hunting knives, rifles, dried meat, biscuits, cornmeal, gunpowder, and gifts for the Indians.

Finally, the time came to leave. The expedition party, numbering close to thirty, boarded the boats. Sacajawea, with Pomp on her back, followed Charbonneau and stepped into one of the pirogues. The captains boarded it as well. Scannon, wagging his tail, scrambled in after them.

As the boats passed by, crowds along both shores waved and called out. Sacajawea waved back. No one aboard the boats, not even Charbonneau, realized how excited she was. She turned her head and whispered to Pomp, "We're going home!"

CHAPTER 8

The Lewis and Clark expedition headed upstream, leaving the villages of the Hidatsas and the Mandans behind. Flat plains, covered with grasses taller than buffalo, stretched to the horizon on both sides of the river.

For the first month, the boats traveled fifteen miles upstream each day. Wide-spreading cottonwood trees along the banks were sprouting pale green leaves. On the prairie beyond, tiny deer mice scurried up and down the tall grasses and searched for seeds.

Late each afternoon, the men set up tents and camped for the night. Nighttime was very cold. Often, in the chilly mornings, the men found ice on their cooking utensils.

As the days passed, they saw fewer trees and shorter grasses. Herds of buffalo, elk, deer, and antelope grazed on the dry, flat plains and hills, from one end of the horizon to the other. Thousands of squirrel-size prairie dogs nervously popped in and out of their burrows.

Early one morning in the middle of May, the air was unusually warm and still. Sacajawea and Charbonneau had just finished eating a breakfast of corn mush, roasted beaver tail, and beaver liver. Captain Clark passed by and greeted them. He was carrying a wooden box under on arm.

"Before the expedition sets off this morning," he said, "I'm going for a little walk to gather plants and insects."

"We could go with you," said Charbonneau. "Sacajawea could tell you about them."

Sacajawea strapped Pomp's cradleboard on her back.

"I will take my digging stick and basket," she said. "We might find wild artichoke roots that mice have hidden. We can bring some back for the men. The roots are very good to eat."

Captain Clark raised his eyebrows.

"The mice hide artichoke roots?" he asked.

"Yes," said Sacajawea, "in old wood. Sometimes close to the river."

The day was becoming very hot. They walked along the base of the bluffs that stretched along both riverbanks.

Every now and then Captain Clark collected plants or insects and put them into his box. When they were almost a mile from camp, Sacajawea spotted a pile of driftwood.

"Those are places for artichoke roots," she said.

She poked the earth around the wood. In a few moments, her sharp digging stick uncovered a horde of roots.

While she was working, Pomp began to fuss.

"The sun is getting in his eyes," she said.

She walked to the base of the bluff, unstrapped the cradleboard, and propped it up in a spot of shade.

"Good," said Captain Clark. "Now Pomp can watch us."

Sacajawea went back to gather the roots. Charbonneau and Captain Clark helped to pick them up. The sky suddenly grew darker, and a hot breeze stirred the air. Several fat rain-drops fell, making dark splotches on the dry ground.

Sacajawea scrambled to her feet. "Rainstorms come fast

on hot days," she said. "They can be very bad."

She ran to get Pomp. Charbonneau and Captain Clark were right behind her. By the time they reached the baby, the rain was pounding down and swirling around their feet. Sacajawea swept up the cradleboard and tried to fasten the soaked leather straps to her back.

"There is no time for that," said Charbonneau. "We must climb up onto the bluff. Floods like this can carry you away!"

Charbonneau hoisted himself onto a rocky ledge. Sacajawea and Captain Clark handed the cradleboard to him. Then they climbed onto the slippery overhang themselves, inching their way along the ledge and huddling beneath it. Below, the river swelled and overflowed its banks. Gradually the swirling waters rose up the side of the bluff. In less than a half hour, the water had reached the ledge.

"We have to climb higher!" Charbonneau cried. As he moved out from beneath the overhang, he lost his balance and dropped the cradleboard into the swirling water.

"Sacajawea!" shouted Charbonneau. "Get him!"

Sacajawea pushed Charbonneau aside and jumped in. She reached out and grabbed the cradleboard before it floated away. Kneeling on the ledge, Captain Clark took Pomp, who was now screaming. He handed the baby to Charbonneau. Then the captain pulled Sacajawea back up.

"Good grief, man," the captain said to Charbonneau. "Why didn't you jump in right away?"

Charbonneau looked down. "I cannot swim," he said.

Sacajawea was dripping wet. Her soaked deerskin leggings and dress clung to her, and her teeth chattered. She peered though the rain at the face of the bluff. It wasn't very high but it was flat, and there was no place to climb. Suddenly

Sacajawea felt something brush against the side of her head. It was a rope dangling from the top of the bluff! She looked up.

"Captain Clark," she cried out. "It's York!"

"Tie the baby on first!" shouted York.

Captain Clark took the cradleboard from Charbonneau and tied it to the end of the rope.

"Ready to go!" he shouted up to York.

York pulled Pomp up to safety. Then, one by one, he pulled up Sacajawea, Charbonneau, and Captain Clark. He pointed to a nearby cave, and they ran inside.

Captain Clark patted York on the back.

"I will be forever grateful to you," he said.

"I was tying up packing cases with rope," said York. "When the skies got dark, I started to look for you. I thought you might need help carrying your specimens back. When it turned into a flash flood, I *knew* you needed me!"

York found some dry wood in a cave and built a fire. Sacajawea took Pomp from the cradleboard.

"He's not too wet," said Captain Clark. "The buffalo hide kept the water out."

Sacajawea sat close to the fire, with Pomp on her lap. But she couldn't stop shaking from both the cold and the terrible thought of almost losing Pomp. Her baby was not going to be like his father—Pomp would learn to swim!

CHAPTER 9

The next morning, Charbonneau shook Sacajawea awake. "What is the matter with you, lying in bed so late?" he asked. "Little Jean-Baptiste wants to eat."

Sacajawea slowly opened her eyes.

"Charbonneau?" she asked. "Is it you?"

"Of course it is Charbonneau," he said. Then he looked at his wife closely and felt her head.

"God of mercy," he said. "You are burning with fever."

Sacajawea closed her eyes, and Charbonneau ran for help.

Sacajawea tried to call after him, but she could not move or make a sound. She had never felt so bad: Her stomach hurt and her head pounded. This trip was not turning out to be good. Little Pomp had almost drowned. And now she herself was lying here worn out, like a rabbit chased by hunters.

Then something terrible occurred to her. Was it possible she might not get better? The idea of never getting back to her homeland filled her with sadness. As she thought about her land, memories wove in and out of her aching head.

Thoughts of home reminded her of Happy Song...the day they gathered pine nuts...the golden eagle...how much she wanted to fly...her wish for her new name.

Men's voices broke into the fuzzy passages of her mind.

"She looks dreadful, so flushed and weak," said Captain Lewis. "We will delay the trip until she feels better."

Their voices faded away, and the words of Old Father came back to her: "Someday you will do something you can't even dream of now. At first you will think it is bad. But it will be good. Wait and see!"

Once, she thought he had been talking about changing her name. Perhaps that was only part of what he meant. Could he have been talking about everything that would happen to her—her capture, her new name, and now this trip?

Maybe the journey would become a good thing after all and she would see her people again. But even so, it would not take care of her greatest sorrow: She had never made her vision quest. She had no guardian spirit to guide her.

Now it was too late for her to make a vision quest. She was married to Charbonneau, and he would tell her she couldn't leave Pomp and him behind to go on such a foolish quest, even for a few days. But without a guardian spirit, her people would never think of her as a true Shoshone woman. She would always remain incomplete.

And then she had a strange and wonderful thought: The journey was proving to be uncertain and dangerous like a true vision quest. Perhaps this very journey might serve as her quest, and at its end, she might find her guardian spirit.

She would be crossing the Mountains of No Summer. They were the mountains the white men called the Rockies, the same mountains where Shoshone boys and girls searched for their guardian spirits. The journey would go on and on to the edge of the earth, where the land met the Never-Ending Waters, which white men called the Pacific Ocean.

A quest was not just a time of danger. In order to prepare the mind, the body must suffer. As her quest drew to its close, Sacajawea would deprive her body of comfort. Then, if she were blessed, her guardian spirit would appear to her at the Never-Ending Waters. She hoped with all her heart that it would be as Happy Song had once said, that her guardian spirit would be a bird.

She fought to get well. Captain Lewis came to visit, holding a quart jar filled with a dark, brown liquid.

"Give this to Sacajawea," he instructed Charbonneau. "It's a brew I've made from chokeberry twigs. She must finish all of it in one hour's time."

"How do you know so much about the plant medicines, Captain Lewis?" he asked.

Captain Lewis smiled.

"My mother taught me," he said. "Back home in Virginia, she was known as an herb doctor. My mother cured everything with plants, from bellyaches to weak legs!"

Sacajawea drank some brew and made a face.

"I know," said Captain Lewis. "It tastes terrible. But I think it will work!"

Sacajawea felt much better by nightfall. She kept all her thoughts about the vision quest to herself. Perhaps it was foolish, this idea that came to her while she was confused with fever. But she was going to do it anyway. She would never tell Charbonneau; he wouldn't understand. But someday, she would tell Pomp!

CHAPTER 10

he next day, Sacajawea was well enough to travel. As she and Charbonneau climbed aboard the largest pirogue, a little breeze slapped the water against its sides. More than a dozen men, acting as oarsmen, were already seated in their positions. George Drouillard, an interpreter and scout, was speaking to Captain Lewis.

"I wrenched my arm last night, sir," Drouillard was explaining. "I wondered if you might have someone take my place as steersman on the boat today."

Charbonneau spoke up. "I will take this man's position."

"Fine, Charbonneau," said Captain Lewis. Then he turned back to speak to Drouillard.

"Captain Clark and I will be walking along the shore for part of the day," he said. "Precious cargo is in your hands."

When they were alone, Sacajawea whispered to Charbonneau.

"Do you know how to do this steering?" she asked.

Charbonneau scowled at her. "Of course I do," he said.

"Man your positions!" shouted Sergeant Gass.

Charbonneau smiled at Sacajawea. "You watch what a fine job I will do," he bragged.

The boat got under sail. The river was not very deep, but the current was swift. All went well until late afternoon, when a violent gust of wind hit the river. The wind caught the sail and tipped the boat dangerously. A light rain began to fall.

The man working the sail brace had it torn right from his hands. "It's a squall!" he shouted. "We're going to capsize!"

From the shore, the captains shouted orders, but their voices were lost in the wind. Charbonneau struggled to steer as water slopped into the slanting boat. "We are done for!" he cried, throwing his hands in the air. "God have mercy!"

"Charbonneau," shouted one of the men. "Take hold and do your duty, or I swear I'll shoot you!"

Several men frantically began to bail out the sinking pirogue with kettles. Sacajawea saw the captains' boxes slide one by one over the deck and into the river.

"The boxes," she called out. "They are washing away!" She leaned over the side and tried to retrieve the bobbing cargo. They floated just beyond reach of her fingertips.

She would have to go in after them with Pomp. There was no other way. Careful to keep Pomp's head above water, she waded over to the drifting boxes.

Before she could reach them, one split open, and dozens of papers scattered over the choppy water. Keeping herself afloat, she grabbed as many as she could and stuffed them into the floating box. She reached the remaining boxes, pushed them back toward the boat, and managed to heave them aboard. Then she pulled herself onto the pirogue.

The squall blew its way down the river. The captains paddled over to the pirogue in a canoe and climbed aboard.

"Sacajawea," said Captain Lewis. "We saw what you did. That was very brave of you. We are grateful."

"What did *she* do?" asked Charbonneau. "I was the one doing all the work!"

"She rescued nearly everything necessary for our purposes," said Captain Lewis. "We are two thousand miles away from any replacements!"

When they got ashore, Sacajawea watched the captains open the soaked boxes and empty the contents on the bank.

"We're very lucky, William. The instruments are safe," said Captain Lewis. "Most of our losses are small. But unfortunately, we've also lost our medicines."

Captain Clark spread out the wet papers and examined his book on botany, filled with exact illustrations of plants. Then he leafed through a book that gave daily locations of the sun, the moon, and the planets.

"What luck!" he exclaimed as he closed the book. "The ephemeris isn't damaged a bit!"

The rest of the explorers, exhausted from fighting the squall, set up camp. They unpacked the bedding and cooked over camp fires that they built along the shore. After supper they relaxed in the light of the glowing fires.

"Come on, Cruzatte," said Captain Lewis, patting one of his men on the back, "let's have a little music."

Peter Cruzatte took out his violin and began to play. Sacajawea sat close by and listened intently. She'd never heard a violin before.

Three of the men got up and began to dance. Scannon, barking excitedly, bounded about their kicking legs. But the squall had tired everybody out, and after a bit, the men turned in for the night and stretched out on the ground in bedrolls.

In his tent, by the light of an oil lamp, Captain Lewis finished writing the accounts of the day in his journal.

"Sacajawea," he said to Captain Clark, "acted with as much strength and intelligence as any man aboard."

"And a lot better than that husband of hers!" said Captain Clark. Scannon barked wildly outside in the dark. "I wonder what he's found now. Probably a raccoon."

A gigantic crash shook the night air, and outside, the men shouted in confusion and alarm.

"Good grief!" said Captain Clark.

In the next seconds, a huge snorting animal charged past their tent. Then it was gone, and the loud drumming of its hoofbeats faded. The only racket left in camp was coming from Pomp, frightened and crying in Sacajawea's arms.

Sergeant Gass opened the captains' tent flap. "Are you two all right?" he asked.

"What in the world was that?" asked Captain Lewis.

"Well, sir," said the sergeant, "you both were almost run down by three thousand pounds of buffalo meat."

"A buffalo!" said Captain Clark.

"It swam across the Missouri," explained Sergeant Gass, "and got itself over the beached pirogues. Then it tore across the camp, barely missing poor Cruzatte in his blanket."

"Is he all right?" Captain Lewis asked, startled.

"He's plenty grateful—Scannon's barking woke him up just before the great shaggy beast got to him," said Sergeant Gass. "He's happiest about his violin. It's still in one piece!"

In her tent, Sacajawea calmed Pomp. Soon, the baby and the rest of the camp slept. After the squall and the rampaging buffalo, everyone had seen enough of that day.

CHAPTER 11

The boats pushed on. With the spring rains, billions of mosquitoes and black flies hatched. They tortured everybody all day and kept them awake at night, buzzing about their ears and stinging their faces and necks.

By the middle of June, the weather stayed hot, and the land along the river was scrubby and dry. And all day long, a hot, dry wind blew. Now the problem was no longer bugs, it was snakes. When the men were on shore, they had to be careful where they stepped: Hidden among the rocks, rattlesnakes waited for the sun to set. Then, in the cool darkness, they slid out into the open and hunted.

Week after week, the white men rowed upriver. As they neared Shoshone country, Sacajawea scanned the flat, rugged land. She knew her people would have left their winter villages. They would be moving from place to place, hunting and fishing.

"No one is out there," she told Captain Clark one day as she peered across the empty plains. It was discouraging. There was no way to tell where her people might be. She turned to search in another direction.

There was nothing new, just the same cliff in the distance

that she'd noticed earlier in the day. But now the boats were drawing closer and she could see it better. She shielded her eyes from the sun and squinted. Nestled at the foot of the cliff was a village—she was sure of it!

"Captain Clark!" called Sacajawea, pointing to the cliff.

"Look at that!" said the captain. "Indian lodges, about a mile away. There must be twenty of them!"

He ordered the men to beach the boats along the river, and he and Captain Lewis went to investigate, taking Charbonneau and Sacajawea with them.

"If the Indians see a woman and child with us," Captain Lewis had explained to the crew, "and we are alone and unarmed, they will know we come in peace."

"And keep Scannon here with you," he added, pointing to his dog. "I don't want him startling anyone."

But as Sacajawea, the captains, and Charbonneau neared the village, they saw that it was empty and had been abandoned long ago. Filled with disappointment, the captains turned around and walked back toward the river. Sacajawea held on to one hope: They would surely find Shoshones when they reached Three Forks—it was such a fine place to fish.

The next morning, the air was hazy, and it stayed that way for several days, making it impossible for Sacajawea to search across the land. One afternoon, at sunset, the haze lifted, and she saw a line of jagged snowcapped forms along the western horizon. She recognized them at once. They were the Mountains of No Summer!

"Look!" she called to Captain Clark, pointing to the mountains far in the distance. The captain hooted aloud.

"All eyes west!" he shouted to his men. "It's the Rockies!"

Sacajawea turned around to hide her tears of joy. With each day, she was nearer to home.

The next afternoon on the river, she could hear a faint roar in the distance. As hours passed, it grew louder.

"I have heard that sound before," she said to Charbonneau. "It is a waterfall. I saw many when I was taken from my home by the Hidatsa warriors."

"We are going to meet a waterfall that crashes down on us?" exclaimed Charbonneau. "I must tell the captains!"

He ran off and told Captain Lewis.

"Don't worry, Charbonneau," said Captain Lewis. "The Mandans warned us about them. We are approaching the great falls. Some of my men went ahead to size up the situation and have returned with a report. The river is beginning to step up. It climbs a series of waterfalls that continues for ten miles upriver. At the great falls, the river is about three hundred yards across and the falls are eighty feet high."

Charbonneau gasped. "How will we get past all these falls?" he asked. "The boats must not get too close. The falls will smash us to bits. We will all be killed!"

Captain Lewis shook his head and sighed to himself. Charbonneau was such an excitable man, he thought.

"We'll have to make camp before we reach the falls," said the captain, "and prepare for a long portage."

"A portage?" exclaimed Charbonneau. "We have to *carry* all these boats over the land? How far? I have done this portage business many times, and boats are very heavy."

Captain Lewis raised his eyes, took a deep breath, and let it out. "Not carry them, Charbonneau," he said. "We have to build wagons and load the canoes onto them. The pirogues are too heavy to pull, so we'll have to leave them behind. We'll replace them by building more canoes after the portage."

Charbonneau shook his head. "This portage business will be very hard."

"You're a strange man, Charbonneau," Captain Lewis said. "First you worry about getting too close to the falls. Now you don't like the idea of a portage. What do you suggest we do? We are not birds. We cannot fly!"

Late that afternoon, still a few miles below the first falls, they made camp.

"There isn't much wood around here to make wagon wheels," Sergeant Gass reported to Captain Lewis. "But there are some good-size cotton trees. We'll cut them down and use thick slices of the trunk for wheels."

"Sounds like a good idea to me," said the captain.

Several men went out to scout the area. Two hours or so later, everybody in the camp heard six rifle shots downriver. Sacajawea, Charbonneau, and the others ran to the shore to see what was happening. In the distance, the men from the scouting party were running full-speed into the water. An enormous reddish-brown bear plunged right in after them. Before Captain Lewis could hold him back, Scannon dashed toward the men and the bear.

"A grizzly!" gasped Captain Lewis. "They've only wounded it. If it catches them, they're dead men." He knew he'd never be able to call Scannon back. The dog was much too excited. But he also knew that if Scannon tangled with the bear, the dog would be killed, too.

The bear threw itself after the men, but halfway across the river it began to slow down. It sank out of sight. Scannon waited on the bank as the exhausted men swam ashore and staggered back to camp.

"Never saw anything like it," said Cruzatte. "That bear must have weighed eight hundred pounds. We shot it six times, and it still came after us. We're lucky to be alive."

He shook his head in wonder. "First a buffalo just about runs me over, and now a grizzly almost finishes me off!"

He took a worn-out moccasin from his pocket and handed it to Captain Lewis. "I picked this up in the woods before the bear appeared. There must be some Indians around here."

The captain took the moccasin from Cruzatte. With a little luck it might have been made by a Shoshone. "Does this belong to your kinsmen?" he asked Sacajawea.

Sacajawea carefully examined the moccasin. Then she shook her head. "No," she said sadly. "This is not a Shoshone moccasin. It must be from someone else."

Captain Lewis sighed deeply. He was just as anxious as Sacajawea to find her people. If they were unable to find some Shoshones, they couldn't borrow horses, and without horses, they couldn't cross the Rockies.

Two nights later, the men finished the wagons and lashed the canoes onto them with strong ropes. At sunup they began to pull the heavy loads overland, past the falls.

Captain Clark walked along the river as close to the falls as possible, making notes and gathering specimens. Sacajawea and Charbonneau went with him. None of them spoke when they reached the Great Falls; its roar drowned out all other sounds. Sacajawea remembered that the Hidatsas had said that the thundering waters were so powerful, the earth shook. They were right. She felt the earth tremble beneath her.

The portage was very difficult. Prickly pear cactus grew close to the ground, and the needle-sharp spines pierced the soles of the men's leather shoes.

Almost daily, one of the wagons broke down. Each time the men repaired a wagon, they had to unload the canoes and supplies. Then they had to reload the wagon after it was fixed. By the end of the portage, the men were worn out and in pain.

"The men are in bad shape and need a rest," Sergeant Gass reported to the captains. "This portage has been the toughest part of the trip. It's taken us ten days to travel eighteen miles. Some poor fellows have infections from the thorns."

"I know," said Captain Clark. "I pulled out seventeen cactus needles from my feet in just one night."

"The men can take a rest for a few days," said Captain Lewis. "I wish I could give them more time, but we must push on. We have to cross the Rockies before winter sets in, and we haven't even found the Shoshones yet."

The men rested for several days. They cleaned and bandaged their wounds, washed their clothes, and swam in the river. Then they got back to work and cut down two large cottonwood trees. They hollowed out both trunks and turned them into dugout canoes to replace the pirogues.

By mid-July, the expedition was on its way up the Missouri again. The land was no longer flat and open. Sacajawea couldn't see the Mountains of No Summer anymore because towering limestone rocks walled in both sides of the river. Carved by millions of years of wind and rain, they stood gleaming white in the sunshine.

The river was shallow, and the canoes often became stranded on sandbars. Some of the men had to wade in the icy waters and work the boats free. The others stood in the canoes and pushed against the riverbottom with long poles.

Late one afternoon, while the men tried to free the boats, the captains walked along the shore to look for plants and animals and to collect samples of the limestone.

"It's like being in a huge cathedral," Captain Clark said. He leaned his head back to see the top of the cliffs. "These canyon walls must be over a thousand feet high."

"We should give them an official name," said Captain Lewis. "What about the Gates of the Mountains?"

"Splendid!" said Captain Clark.

After a few more days of travel, tall cliffs no longer walled in the river. Sacajawea resumed her search and scanned the dry land for signs of people.

On a hot afternoon in late July, the expedition reached the river's headwaters, where three smaller rivers came together to become one. Sacajawea recognized the place at once. They had arrived at Three Forks!

"It is here I was captured," she said to Charbonneau. "Happy Song and I were gathering cattails." As she looked around, memories of that dreadful day came back, and she could no longer tell him about it.

Captain Lewis spoke to her. "These three rivers fork out in different directions. They wind so much it's hard to tell which one flows toward Shoshone country. Do you know which river we should follow?"

Sacajawea looked closely at the three forks of water. Each one looked the same.

"I do not know," she said. "I cannot tell which one leads to my people."

"Why aren't any of your people at Three Forks?" Captain Lewis asked. "I thought you said they would be here fishing." He frowned. "I am very disappointed no one's here. We have to find them, Sacajawea. We must get horses."

"The fishing may not be good this year," she explained.

"Everyone may be out hunting on the plains." Didn't he realize that she was disappointed, too?

The expedition set up camp at Three Forks. The captains and their men spent more than a week scouting the area, trying to decide which fork to take. They finally decided on the one that flowed to the northwest. The captains named it the Jefferson River in honor of their president.

The men broke camp, loaded the canoes, and rowed up the Jefferson River. The days were very hot, with no breezes. Sacajawea continued to search. Early one morning, she thought she saw smoke in the distance, but she wasn't sure. Late in the afternoon, she spotted a familiar large rock in the distance. Against the sky, it looked like the head of a huge beaver. She let out a yelp of joy that startled Charbonneau, who was standing next to her.

"Sacajawea," he asked in alarm, "are you all right?"

"We are on the right river," she said, clapping her hands. "There is Beaverhead Rock. I have told you about it. I passed it many times on the way to Three Forks with my family. Oh, Charbonneau, maybe we will find them soon!"

Captain Lewis overheard the good news and felt encouraged for the first time in many days.

"I think we should set up camp right here," he said. "It's time we stopped for the day, anyway. It's too hot to row much more. That smoke you thought you saw earlier might have been a Shoshone camp fire. First thing tomorrow, Drouillard and I will take several men out on a scouting party. With some luck we'll run into someone."

"I would like to go with them," Sacajawea said to Charbonneau. "I could help them look."

"That's fine with me," said Captain Lewis. He was sorry

he'd been so harsh with her at Three Forks. "What do you say, Charbonneau?"

Charbonneau was disagreeable. "No! It is too hot to go walking around. Sacajawea will get sick in this heat."

"Please, Charbonneau," began Sacajawea. "I wish to go."

"*No!*" he repeated. "You do not go!"

Captain Clark was shocked by Charbonneau's behavior. Couldn't the man see how much his wife wanted to go? But he knew there was no arguing with Charbonneau.

He patted Sacajawea on her shoulder. "Don't worry," he told her. "Drouillard is an excellent scout. If there are people out there, he'll find them."

The next morning at daybreak, the scouting party left. Sacajawea watched them cross the plains. She knew she should be with them. She knew she could have helped.

Several days passed, and the scouting party was nowhere in sight. Sacajawea was bathing Pomp in the river when Charbonneau hurried up to her. "They are coming back," he said. She quickly dried off Pomp and put him inside his cradleboard. Charbonneau helped her tie it on her back. "I told you," he said with a smile. "You did not have to go for that long, hot walk."

Sacajawea peered anxiously across the flat, grassy plain. A group of men on horseback were riding straight toward the camp. As they got closer, she could see them clearly. They were Shoshones.

Sacajawea ran to meet the horsemen. More than a dozen Shoshone braves rode into camp on white horses with brown markings. Drouillard, also one of the riders, led three riderless horses joined together by a long rope. He waved to Sacajawea.

Anxiously, she looked from face to face but did not recognize any of the braves.

"As you see, we had good luck," Druoillard told Captain Clark. "We found a Shoshone camp. Captain Lewis is waiting for us there. He wants you to bring Sacajawea along to interpret in a council with the chief."

As soon as she heard Drouillard's words, Sacajawea untied one of the horses and mounted it.

"Wait," said Charbonneau, running up to her. "You cannot ride with little Jean-Baptiste on your back. He might bounce off!"

"I'm sure she knows what she's doing, Charbonneau," said Captain Clark.

He smiled at Sacajawea. "Why don't you take a little ride by yourself while we get ready to go?" he suggested to her.

Sacajawea grinned back at him.

Without looking at Charbonneau, she kicked the horse with her heels and cantered off. Before her capture, she had ridden horses all the time. Now, feeling the horse's strength beneath her, she remembered how much she loved to ride. She said to Pomp, "I will teach you to be a fine rider someday. Then you will be a real Shoshone boy!"

When she rode back to camp, Captain Clark was almost ready to go. Charbonneau was already on horseback, and a few minutes later, they all followed the Shoshone braves and Drouillard onto the plains. After an hour's ride, they arrived at the Shoshone camp.

"I will take Captain Clark into the council tent," Drouillard said to Charbonneau. "They will call for Sacajawea in a little while."

Sacajawea could hardly wait. Perhaps the chief knewher family....

CHAPTER 12

aptain Clark followed Drouillard into a large circular tent.
The Shoshone chief and Captain Lewis were seated on two
white robes. The chief was a strong-looking man of fewer
than thirty years. He was dressed in deerskin and wore a necklace of grizzly bear claws. When he saw Captain Clark, he
motioned to a white robe lying next to him. The captain sat
down, and the chief tied six pearly shells in the white man's hair.
Captain Clark nodded his head in thanks.

"Greetings, Clark," said Captain Lewis, who was wearing
shells in his hair as well. "The Shoshones have been very cordial
to me. I believe these shells are tokens of friendship. Drouillard
says before any official council with Indians can begin, we must
smoke a pipe of peace with the chief."

"Of course," said Captain Clark.

Together the three men shared a long-stemmed pipe. It
was fashioned from a hollow reed and attached to a bowl of pol-
ished green stone. When they finished smoking, Captain Lewis
sent for Sacajawea, who hurried right in.

"Sacajawea," said Captain Lewis. "We would like you to
speak to the chief for us. First of all, I'm not sure I'm pro-
nouncing his name correctly."

Sacajawea knew how to pronounce his name—it was Cameahwait! She ran over to the chief and threw her arms around him. "Cameahwait is my brother!" she said to the captains before her voice broke and she began to sob.

Cameahwait rose and stared at Sacajawea. As he recognized her, he hugged her to him. "Grass Maiden, is it you?"

Captain Clark hastened to his feet. "Come, Meriwether," he said. "I think we should leave them alone for a while."

Cameahwait gently wiped the tears from his sister's cheeks. "Let me look at you," he said. "My eyes see you, but I cannot believe you are really here."

Sacajawea smiled. "Old Father was right," she said. "He said you would be a chief." She looked at his necklace and felt proud of her brother. To have the honor of wearing the claws of a grizzly bear, she knew he must have fought the great animal all alone and won.

"What is that name the white men call you?" asked Cameahwait.

"Sacajawea," she explained. "The Hidatsas changed my name to Bird Woman."

"It is a good name for you," said Cameahwait. "You always loved birds, I remember."

He turned Sacajawea around and peeked at Pomp, who was wide awake in his cradleboard. "Is this your baby?" he asked.

"Yes," Sacajawea said proudly. "His name is Pompey. The white men and I call him Pomp. My husband, Charbonneau, calls him Jean-Baptiste."

"So many names!" said Cameahwait. He looked at Pompey closely. "He looks a lot like me."

Sacajawea laughed. Cameahwait hadn't changed.

"Where are mother and father?" Sacajawea asked.

Cameahwait's smile vanished. "Grass Maiden," he said. "Two winters after you left, there was a terrible sickness in the lodges. Many died. Mother and Father..."

"They are not alive?" gasped Sacajawea.

Cameahwait slowly shook his head. "Old Father, too."

Sacajawea hid her face in her hands. She had not expected to see Old Father again; he was a very old man. But her parents! All this time when she imagined what they were doing, they were not even there.

Cameahwait put his arm around her. "They believed you would come back. Old Father told us so."

For some reason, this made Sacajawea feel better. Then she thought of her friend. "And Happy Song?" she asked fearfully. "Is she..."

Cameahwait smiled. "She is fine," he said. "She has two little daughters. Now tell me, little sister, what do the white men want?"

Sacajawea told him what she knew.

"I can sell them some horses," said Cameahwait. "But it will be a hard trip over the Mountains of No Summer. You can wait here for the horses. I'll send Toby to show the white men the way. He is my best guide."

"You may send Toby," said Sacajawea, "but I am going. I want to see the Never-Ending Waters." She would not tell him about her vision quest. He might think her foolish.

Cameahwait could tell she wouldn't change her mind. "I wish you well," he said. He smiled to himself. Grass Maiden was still the same—full of spirit and a little bit stubborn.

"Let us begin the conference now," he said. "Tell the white men to come in."

The conference lasted more than three hours. By the end of the meeting, the white men had bought more than thirty horses. They presented Cameahwait with a silver Jefferson medal engraved on the front with a portrait of their president. On the back, a crossed peace pipe and tomahawk were pictured above hands clasped in friendship.

As soon as Sacajawea stepped from the tent, she saw a woman with two little girls waiting outside. "Happy Song!" she cried, and ran up to her.

"Grass Maiden," said Happy Song, blinking back tears of joy. "I could not trust my ears when I was told that you were here. I cannot wait to hear what happened to you!"

Sacajawea sat in the shade of a tree with her dear friend and told of her life with the Hidatsas and her marriage to Charbonneau. She was in the middle of telling how she was going to the Never-Ending Waters with the white men when an old man approached them.

"Grass Maiden," he said, smiling a grin that showed three teeth missing. "You are back. I already have two wives, but I see no reason not to have one more." It was Blue Feather, the man her parents had chosen to be her husband.

"Blue Feather," said Sacajawea. "I have a husband and a baby son. I cannot marry you." At that moment she knew she could not return to the life she'd left behind. Her place was with Charbonneau and Pomp.

Blue Feather did not seem to mind. "All right," he said. Then he walked away.

Happy Song giggled. "Can you imagine being married to Blue Feather?" she asked.

Sacajawea laughed. "No," she said. "Now tell me, Happy Song, what have *you* been doing while I was away?"

CHAPTER

13

Once they had horses, the captains wanted to leave the Shoshone camp as soon as possible so that they could cross the Rocky Mountains before winter set in.

The first week on the trail, the weather was good and the horses had no trouble keeping their footing along the narrow ledges. By the second week, they had climbed seven thousand feet to the top of the Rocky Mountains.

One morning, Captain Lewis noticed four long ax cuts high up on a tree trunk. They were at least two inches deep.

"Look, William," he said to Captain Clark. "Some fellow's been here before us, marking the trail with an ax! But the cuts are ten feet above the ground. I wonder how he reached up there. I guess he stood on his horse's back."

"Ask Toby about these ax cuts," he said to Sacajawea. "Maybe we can catch up with whoever made them."

When she spoke to Toby, Captain Lewis saw the Shoshone guide smile. "Toby says you do not want to travel with the one who made these marks," Sacajawea reported to the captain. "The great grizzly bear made them. To keep his claws sharp like a knife, he stands up and scratches a tree."

"Great heavens," said Captain Clark, looking about.

"Those marks are fresh. For all we know they were just made!"

"Toby also warns that it will soon snow," Sacajawea added. "He says the horses might slide down the cliff."

By noon, the snow was falling fast, and the jittery horses picked their way slowly over the whitened rocks.

The snow fell hard for the rest of the day. Sacajawea's feet were so cold she couldn't feel them. By late afternoon, the snow turned to sleet. Then it started to hail. Some hailstones were as big as her fist! Holding a heavy buffalo robe over her head and shoulders, Sacajawea tried to keep Pomp dry in his cradleboard. She worried about him, her poor little son, sobbing with fright and shivering from the cold. The mountains were a terrible place for him to be. But despite her fears for his safety, she knew she must make this journey to the Never-Ending Waters. To be a good mother, she had to be a Shoshone woman with a guardian spirit, a spirit that would guide her wisely all the rest of her life.

When the weather finally cleared, it was nighttime. The frozen mountains glowed in the brightness of the moon and the stars. One of the men spotted a wandering mountain goat and aimed his rifle at it. At once, Charbonneau grabbed the man's arm and stopped him from shooting.

"What's the matter now, Charbonneau?" asked Captain Clark. "We could use a little meat around here."

"Captain Clark," said Charbonneau, keeping his voice low. "You must be quiet and listen to me. I know I am not the good swimmer or the good man at the keel of the boat. But I have lived many years in the mountains of Canada, and this I know: The loud sound of a rifle can shake the snow on the mountainside and—whoosh!—there is a terrible avalanche. Thousands of tons of snow can come crashing down the mountain to sweep away the tall trees, the heavy rocks, and us!"

"Charbonneau is right," said Drouillard, keeping his voice low as well. "Conditions are just right for an avalanche. We must keep going until we are in a safer place. We also must not talk, as the slightest sounds can echo and cause dangerous vibrations."

"The horses," whispered Charbonneau. "We must try to keep them as quiet as possible." He turned to Sacajawea. "And Jean-Baptiste," he said. "Do not let him cry!"

How did he expect her to do that? Sacajawea wondered. She would just have to hope that their son would be quiet.

For the next two hours, as everybody silently crossed the mountain pass, Sacajawea worried. What if Pomp let out a yowl and caused the snow to tumble down on them?

But the baby slept, and they reached safety. For the remainder of the night, they took shelter in a cave.

Just before dawn, Sacajawea awoke to the rumble of thunder. But instead of coming from the skies, it came from the mountain. "Avalanche!" someone shouted.

Sacajawea grabbed Pomp and held him close to her. What should she do? There was no place to go. But, in seconds, everything was quiet, and they were still alive.

Sacajawea looked across the mountain pass, and in the early morning light, she saw what had happened. The pass they had crossed the night before was buried in snow.

The captains were standing nearby.

"Charbonneau was right," she heard Captain Lewis say. "For once, that annoying man knew what he was talking about. If we'd spent the night in the pass, that avalanche would have finished us off!"

Sacajawea felt sad. The captains did not understand her

Charbonneau. He was not as smart as the captains, and, it was true, he got upset easily, was bossy, and boasted a lot. But he always tried to do the right thing. He *thought* he was being a good husband and father.

Just then Charbonneau came up to her. She had never seen him look so happy.

"You see," he said to Sacajawea, pointing to his chest with one finger. "Charbonneau, he is pretty good to have around!"

For the next few days, they made their way down the western slopes, leaving the freezing weather and snow on the mountains' heights. As they climbed down lower and lower, the air grew warmer. The trip over the Rockies had taken two weeks. Everyone was exhausted and hungry.

"Clark," said Captain Lewis. "We've got to get some food into these men. Why don't you take Toby and some of the hunters and bring us back something to eat?"

"Fine," said Captain Clark. "We'll leave now."

Toby guided Captain Clark and the hunters through a dense pine forest. When they came out of the dark woods, they found a wide prairie spread before them.

"What a magnificent place," said Captain Clark. Then he noticed some women in the distance. They seemed to be gathering something from the ground.

In sign language he asked Toby, "Who are they?"

"Nez Perce women," Toby indicated. "Gathering camas roots—to eat."

Captain Clark thought for a minute or two. He knew the expedition would have to leave their horses behind while they traveled by river to the Pacific. He also knew they had to build some dugout canoes to take them there. Perhaps the Nez Perce people could help them.

Captain Clark spoke again in sign to Toby. "I would like to meet with their chief."

At that moment three boys appeared on the plain, chasing one another on horseback. Toby called to them.

Toby spoke to the boys, and they pointed across the prairie. Then he reported in sign language to Captain Clark. "Their great chief is away with his warriors. They will lead you to their camp."

When Captain Clark arrived at the camp, he traded with the Nez Perces. "Take this food to Captain Lewis," he instructed one of his hunters. "After the men have eaten and gotten back some of their strength, lead them here to us."

Two days later, a Nez Perce brave guided Clark and his men down the river to find another village. There they found Twisted Hair, the great chief, fishing.

Twisted Hair greeted Captain Clark with enthusiasm. With his son and Captain Clark, Chief Twisted Hair rode across the open plain back to his camp. At sundown, Captain Lewis and the rest of the party joined them.

Chief Twisted Hair agreed to keep the horses. His people would watch over them until the expedition came back.

"The captains are fortunate," Sacajawea said to Charbonneau. "The Nez Perce are horse people like the Shoshones. Horses are a part of their lives, and they take good care of them."

Soon a crowd of people gathered around to see the white men. The captains thanked Chief Twisted Hair and his people and presented them with the Jefferson medals, American flags, handkerchiefs, knives, and tobacco. Chief Twisted Hair gave salmon and camas roots to the captains. He took a bit of charcoal and, on a smooth piece of elk skin, drew a map of two rivers that would lead them to the Big River.

The Nez Perce men showed the white men a better and quicker way to make dugout canoes. Instead of hollowing out tree trunks with axes, they burned them out. The explorers built five large canoes and a smaller one to use for scouting. They were now ready to make the final part of their trip.

This time the river travel was very fast. Using Twisted Hair's map, the captains followed the two smaller rivers that led to the Columbia. It was the opposite of traveling up the Missouri. On that river, the men had struggled upstream, against the current, and often had to pull the boats along. Now the canoes were going downstream and were being pushed from behind by the rushing water. The currents were often very strong, and it took all of the men's strength to keep the canoes from tipping over or being torn apart on the rocks.

Sacajawea held on tightly as the canoes spun in and out of churning rapids. The last time she had traveled on the Big River, it had been in her imagination, flying over it when she was little. But now that she was *really* in the waters, she worried that she might be spilled overboard. She remembered her father's words: "Our strongest canoes were tossed and sucked down into the whirlpools as if they were floating leaves."

As the Big River neared the sea, it grew rougher and widened to three miles from shore to shore. Choppy waves bounced the canoes about, and many of the men became seasick. The air was damp and misty most of the time. And the trees were the tallest Sacajawea had ever seen. They looked like pine trees but were much bigger. It would take almost twenty people standing in a circle and holding hands to reach around the great trunks. In the woods were villages with houses built of logs cut from the huge trees. Here and there,

Sacajawea saw tall poles with painted heads of animals carved on them.

Sacajawea watched people fishing for salmon along the shore. Sometimes the banks were glutted with bodies of salmon that had swum upriver from the sea to lay their eggs to die.

Then, at last, one morning she heard Captain Lewis speak the words she'd been waiting to hear for months. "Well, Clark," he said, "we should reach the Pacific soon."

Soon! She knew what she must do. She must stop eating. Shoshones fasted to prepare for their vision quest, and she would do the same.

That evening, Charbonneau noticed she hadn't touched her meal. "Are you ill?" he asked.

"No," she replied. "I cannot explain why I do not eat. Please do not ask me why."

Charbonneau shook his head.

As the days went on, Sacajawea felt weaker, and by the third night, she didn't know if she could hold out much longer. At camp that evening, Captain Lewis made an announcement to his men. "As you know, we have reached the bay of the Pacific Ocean," he said. "The sounds you hear are the waves pounding the shore. I want you to take note of this date. It is November 16, 1805. We have traveled over four thousand miles, and tomorrow morning, we will stand together on the shore of the Pacific Ocean."

That night, Sacajawea waited until Charbonneau was snoring. Then she put Pomp, asleep in his cradleboard, next to him. Careful to not wake Scannon, she tiptoed through the quiet camp and, following the sounds of the Never-Ending Waters, stole into the night.

CHAPTER 14

The moon was out, but the fog was thick, and Sacajawea could barely see. In the darkness, she stubbed one of her bare toes on a sharp rock and cried out in pain. She'd left her moccasins and warm buffalo robe back in camp. In order to deprive her body of as many comforts as possible, all she wore was a thin deerskin dress. Three days of fasting had left her light-headed and weak, and as she stumbled through the cold night, she thought she might faint.

She walked for at least three hours. Now the sounds of the Never-Ending Waters were very loud. She had never heard such noises—crashing waters that would come and then go, over and over again.

At times Sacajawea felt confused and didn't know where to step next. If she became lost and fell into the sea, she would not be found. And Charbonneau would not know why she had gone away. He would think she didn't like being his wife or a mother to his son.

Little by little, the moon crossed the heavens, leaving no light at all. Sacajawea could tell by the sound of the waves that she was very close to the edge of a cliff. Because she couldn't see in front of her, she would have to crawl and feel her way along the ground. On her hands and knees, she crept over the rocks. When, at last, she put her hand down and there was no ground beneath it, she knew she could go no farther.

Slowly Sacajawea rose and stepped back from the edge. The waves, crashing against the rocky cliffs, drenched her from head to foot with icy spray. She licked her lips and tasted salt. She waited. Would her guardian spirit come to her?

She was unsteady and swayed from exhaustion. She peered into the black starless sky but saw nothing there. Her eyes filled with tears, and her heart was heavy with sadness. She had been a fool to do this. She would never have a guardian spirit. How could she have thought otherwise? This trip with the white men was no real vision quest. It was just something she had made up.

Behind her, the sun slowly rose. Now, instead of blackness before her, there was a gray mist. She stared into the mist, trying to see. Her heart jumped. What was that? Had she seen something? No. But wait, there it was again. A flicker of white. In a few moments, it became clear to her. She'd seen a small white bird! Was it her guardian spirit, or just a bird flying in the air? How could she tell?

Without knowing why, Sacajawea closed her eyes and held out her arms. In a few moments, she felt a soft fluttering on her fingers. The bird had come to her and landed in her hands! She knew this must be a sign. She had met her guardian spirit, and to her great joy, it had come to her as a bird!

The bird looked at her and opened its wings wide. Then it flew toward the morning sky. Sacajawea turned her back to the sea and faced the land of the sunrise. She had to hurry back now. Charbonneau and Pomp were waiting for her.

EPILOG

This book is a historical novel. Some of it is true, and some of it tells the way things might have been.

If you look at a map of the United States as it is today, you can find Sacajawea's birthplace. It is said she was born around 1784 in Idaho on the eastern side of the Rocky Mountains. Her family was fishing in Montana when she was kidnapped. Hidatsa warriors took her to their village near present-day Bismarck, North Dakota.

Sacajawea, Charbonneau, and Pomp spent the winter with the Lewis and Clark expedition at the Pacific Ocean at the border between Oregon and Washington. In the spring of 1806, they returned east with the expedition and went back to live in their cabin near the Mandan village.

No one really knows much about Sacajawea's childhood or how long she lived. Some stories say she died a few years after the expedition. Others say she lived to be a very old woman and died in Shoshone country.

The territory explored by the Lewis and Clark expedition, as well as the rest of the present-day United States, was the home of the many peoples we now collectively call Native Americans. As this northwestern part of the United States was settled by those who followed Lewis and Clark, the Native Americans were killed or forced to move from the lands that had been theirs for thousands of years.